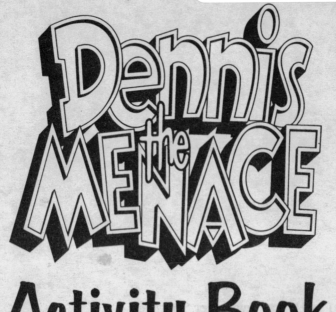

Activity Book

From the Screenplay by John Hughes

A Parachute Press Book

Troll Associates

Written by Devra Newberger Speregen
Designed by Susan Herr
Illustrated by Jerry Zimmerman

The Town Terror!

It's summertime, and the towns-people are looking forward to a nice, quiet summer. But someone's been making a lot of noise on his bicycle at six o'clock every morning! To find out who it is, cross out all the **Q**'s, **X**'s, **Y**'s, and **Z**'s.

Q X D Q Z E Z
N X Y N Y Q I
Y S Z X M X I
T Z Q Z C Y Y
Q H X Y Q E X
Z Y X Q L L Z

Answer:

D E N N I S

M I T C H E L L

Dennis & Company

Dennis sure knows a lot of people! Can you find all his friends and family in the word search below? Look up, down, forward, backward, and diagonally in the puzzle. Circle all the names you find.

ALICE (his mom)

HENRY (his dad)

GEORGE WILSON (his neighbor)

MARTHA WILSON (his neighbor)

MARGARET (a yucky girl)

JOEY (his best friend)

GUNTHER (a neighborhood kid)

RUFF (his dog)

```
N O S L I W E G R O E G
T D B R A N W B R G R U
E H S B R R U F F A S N
R X Z O O H A D M S P T
A J O E Y U N B V E R H
G N V X R O U T C L P E
R S D F N K H I C F T R
A B B K E E L L U R Q Q
M A R T H A W I L S O N
```

Boy's Best Friend

Dennis's special friend is his dog, Ruff. Can you put the names of the following types of dogs in their correct spaces in the puzzle on page 7? We've filled in the first one to get you started.

4 letters
MUTT

5 letters
BOXER
HUSKY

6 letters
AFGHAN
BEAGLE
POODLE

7 letters
POINTER
TERRIER

8 letters
LABRADOR
SHEEPDOG

9 letters
DALMATIAN
GREAT DANE

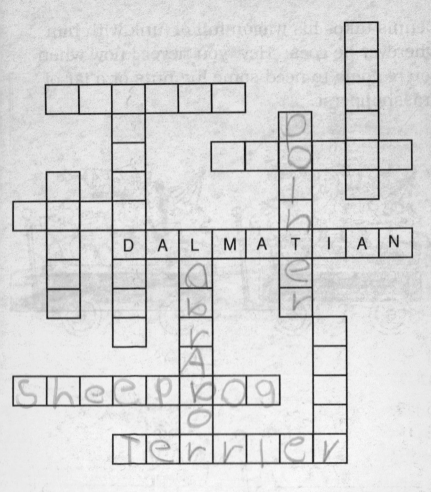

What's in the Wagon?

Dennis takes his wagon full of junk with him wherever he goes. Hey, you never know when you're going to need some lug nuts or a jar of grasshoppers!

Can you find the two wagons of junk that look exactly alike?

Good Morning, Mr. Wilson!

Dennis has been out all morning searching for more junk to add to his collection. Follow his bicycle through town and pick up the letters as you go.

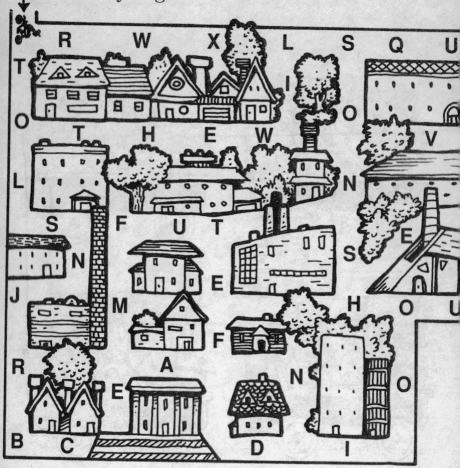

Write each letter in order in the blank spaces
below to find out where Dennis is going now.

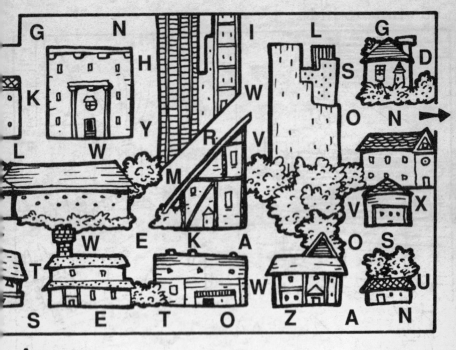

Answer:

__ __   __ __ __ __

__ __ __ __ __ __ __ ,

__ __ __ __ __ __   __ __ __ __ __

__ __ .   __ __ __ __ __ __ __ !

Where's Mr. Wilson?

George Wilson can tell that trouble is coming—he can hear Dennis heading home on his bicycle from way across town! Luckily he still has time to hide.

These two pictures may look alike—but look again! Can you find eight places where they are different?

Open Wide!

Dennis makes so much noise, he always gives Mr. Wilson a headache. Connect the dots to find out what Dennis uses to help Mr. Wilson take an aspirin.

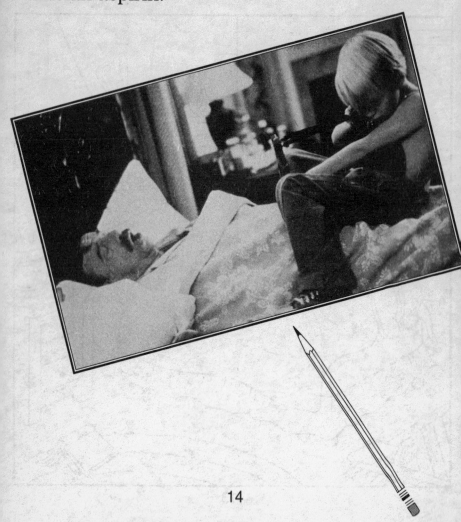

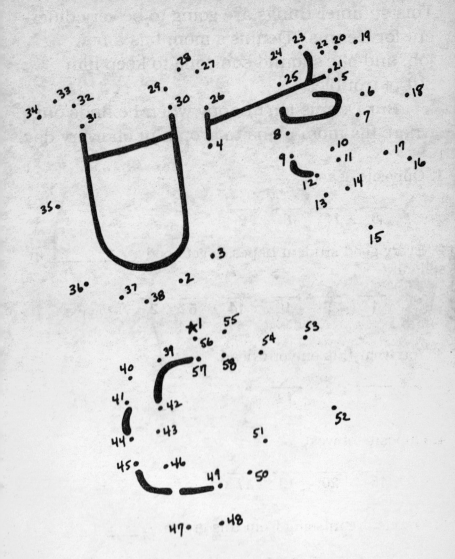

Oh, No! Anything But That!

This summer things are going to be very different for Dennis. Dennis's mom has a new job, and she's found someone to keep him out of trouble!

But Dennis isn't happy when he finds out where his mom plans to drop him off every day.

1. Opposite of cool.

$\overline{}$ $\overline{}$ $\overline{}$ $\overline{}$
 8   11   6   9

2. Every good student hopes to get good _____ in school.

$\overline{}$ $\overline{}$ $\overline{}$ $\overline{}$ $\overline{}$ $\overline{}$
 1   3   10   14   5   2

3. You wear this on your head.

$\overline{}$ $\overline{}$ $\overline{}$
 4   7   12

4. Opposite of west.

$\overline{}$ $\overline{}$ $\overline{}$ $\overline{}$
 15   20   13   17

5. Vowels are missing from this group. A ___ I ___ ___.

$\overline{}$ $\overline{}$ $\overline{}$
 21   19   22

To find out where this will be, fill in the blanks below each clue. Then copy the numbered letters into the spaces below by matching the numbers.

Where will Dennis be spending his summer days?

Answer:

$\overline{20}$ $\overline{12}$ $\overline{9}$ $\overline{10}$ $\overline{3}$ $\overline{1}$ $\overline{7}$ $\overline{6}$ $\overline{15}$ $\overline{17}$

$\overline{8}$ $\overline{11}$ $\overline{14}$ $\overline{21}$ $\overline{13}$, $\overline{4}$ $\overline{19}$ $\overline{22}$ $\overline{2}$ $\overline{5}$!

Yuck!

Dennis's best friend Joey has to stay at Margaret's every afternoon, too. He hates playing with Margaret! Help Joey escape to the tree house before Margaret kisses him—don't run into any lips!

Start

End

The Great Summer Project

What will Dennis, Margaret, and Joey do all summer? Dennis has a great idea! Connect the dots by twos (2, 4, 6, 8, and so on) to see what it is.

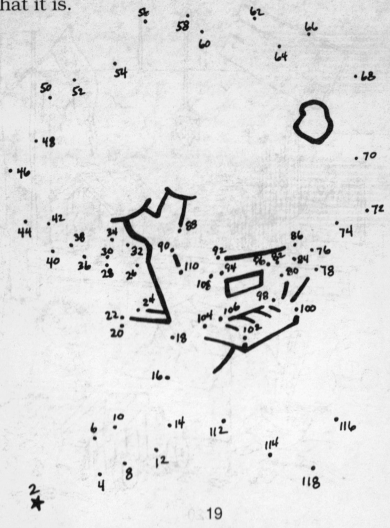

Memory Challenge

Every afternoon Dennis, Margaret, and Joey go out to Turley's Woods to fix up their tree-house fort. They want it to look really cool!

Look carefully at the picture on these pages for one minute. Then turn the page and see how much you can remember about it.

Memory Challenge

How many questions can you answer without peeking at the picture you just studied?

1. How many of Margaret's dolls are in the tree-house fort?_____

2. How many boxes are there? _____

3. How many windows are there?_____

4. Which toy below isn't in the tree house?
A doll. A kite. A truck.

5. Which tool isn't in the tree house?
A hammer. A saw. A wrench.

6. Which truck is on the floor of the tree house?
A dump truck.   A fire engine.   A gas truck.

7. Where did Dennis build a birdhouse?

_____

8. What time is on the broken clock?_____

A Scary-Looking Dude!

It's nighttime, and everyone in town is fast asleep—except a suspicious-looking stranger who's about to make trouble! Use the secret code to figure out the villain's name.

CODE:

A=Z	G=T	M=N	S=H	Y=B
B=Y	H=S	N=M	T=G	Z=A
C=X	I=R	O=L	U=F	
D=W	J=Q	P=K	V=E	
E=V	K=P	Q=J	W=D	
F=U	L=O	R=I	X=C	

ANSWER:

G S V

N B H G V I B

N Z M

R H

H D R G X S Y O Z W V

H Z N.

Where's Baby Louise?

Something strange is happening. Baby Louise, Margaret's favorite doll, has been doll-napped! To find out who took her, first circle all the toys listed on page 25 in the word search below. Look up, down, forward, backward, and diagonally in the puzzle.

S	D	O	M	I	N	O	E	S	W
S	R	E	K	C	E	H	C	I	T
C	R	A	Y	O	N	S	C	M	E
R	U	B	B	E	R	B	A	L	L
H	J	L	B	L	A	R	S	D	C
P	A	O	E	S	B	A	D	M	Y
O	C	C	T	L	O	O	R	K	C
T	K	K	E	B	L	A	A	B	I
Y	S	S	L	O	U	O	C	I	B
S	E	L	Z	Z	U	P	D	S	E

MARBLES
JACKS
RUBBER BALL
DOLL
TOP
CRAYONS
BLOCKS
CHECKERS
DOMINOES
CARDS
BICYCLE
PUZZLES

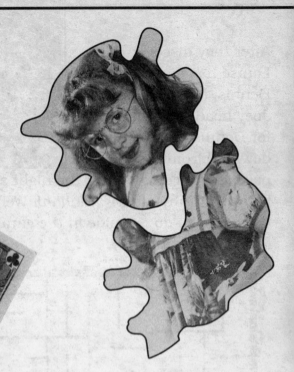

Now put the remaining uncircled letters in the order they appear in the blank spaces below.

Answer:

— — — — — — — —

— — — — — —

— — — — — — — —!

His Little Prints!

After they discover Baby
Louise has disappeared,
Dennis, Margaret, and
Joey head for home. But
for Dennis things only go
downhill from there. His
parents are going out for the night and leaving him with
Polly, the baby-sitter! *Aaahhh!* Well, there's only one
thing he can do . . . hide in the garage! Can you help
Polly find Dennis?

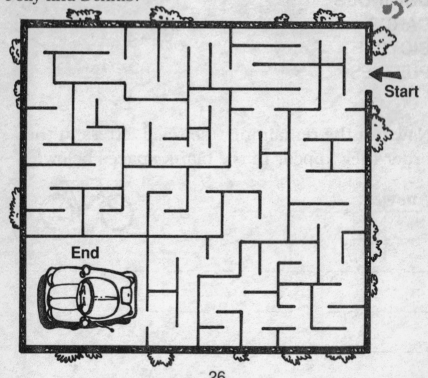

Start

End

Tool Time!

Dennis is searching the garage for some neat stuff to put in the tree house. Can you fit all the things he found into the puzzle? We've filled in the first one to help you get started.

3 letters	4 letters	5 letters	6 letters
AXE	WIRE	PAINT	HAMMER
SAW	FILE	NAILS	WRENCH
	PICK	CLAMP	PLIERS

N A I L S

Mr. Wilson's Chicken!

Why will Mr. Wilson be surprised when he takes a bite of his barbecued chicken?

To find out, take the words in the numbered boxes and put them in the matching numbered spaces below.

7 AND	19 WILSON'S	2 SPRAYED	14 IN	12 IT
18 MR.	8 INTO	11 BACKYARD	15 A	3 PAINT
4 OVER	20 DINNER	5 HIS	9 MR.	13 LANDED
10 WILSON'S	1 DENNIS	16 GLOB	17 ON	6 FENCE

Answer:

_____ _____ _____ _____ _____
  1   2   3   4   5

_____ _____ _____ _____ _____
  6   7   8   9   10

_____. _____ _____ _____ _____
  11   12   13   14   15

_____ _____ _____ _____ _____!
  16   17   18   19   20

Poor Polly!

Polly has had a wild night baby-sitting for the town menace! Use the clues to fill in the puzzle. When you're done, the letters in the shaded boxes will spell out Polly's last message to the Mitchells.

CLUES

1. You can listen to music on a car _____.

2. 25¢ coin.

3. Opposite of empty.

4. Six-stringed instrument.

5. It glitters in the night sky.

Answer:

_____   _____ _____ _____ _____!

The Whole Tooth!

Oops! Dennis has accidentally broken Mr. Wilson's dentures! And wouldn't you know it—today's the day Mr. Wilson is being photographed for the town newspaper with his rare garden plant.

Use the code to find out what Dennis uses to "fix" Mr. Wilson's teeth.

CODE:

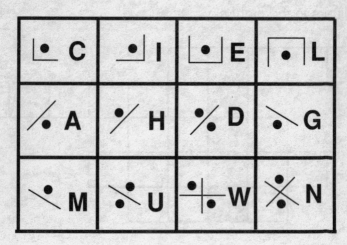

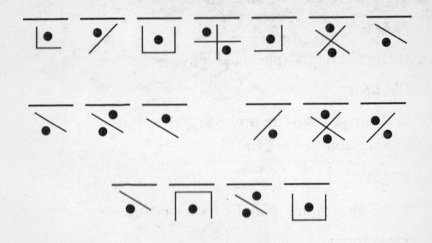

Bad Guy Beware!

Meanwhile, way across town, Switchblade Sam is still up to no good. After doll-napping Baby Louise, he's moved on to stealing bigger things. Unscramble the letters to find out what he's stolen so far!

1. At the jewelry store he stole . . .

   DNMODIAS ◯ ◯ __ __ __ ◯ __ __

2. At the bank he stole . . .

   SACH ◯ __ ◯ ◯

3. At the hardware store he stole . . .

   SOTOL __ __ __ ◯ __

4. At the fruit store he stole an . . .

   PLAPE __ __ __ __ ◯

5. At the zoo he pickpocketed a man's . . .

   TWLLAE __ __ __ ◯ __ __

6. At the restaurant he broke into the cash register and took all the . . .

   NOEMY ◯ __ ◯ __ __

7. At the electronics shop he took a color . . .

   VTLSOEEIIN ◯ __ __ ◯ __ ◯ __ __ __

Now unscramble all the circled letters to discover who Switchblade Sam's next victim will be. We've filled in two of the letters to get you started.

Answer:

__ __ __ **N** __ __

__ __ **T** __ __ __ __

Help Wanted!

Henry and Alice Mitchell have a giant problem. Since their son is the biggest little troublemaker in the neighborhood, they can't seem to find......

—   — — — — —

— — — — — —

— — — — — - — — — — — — —

— — —

— — — — — — !

Go around the circle twice, writing every other letter in the blank spaces above.

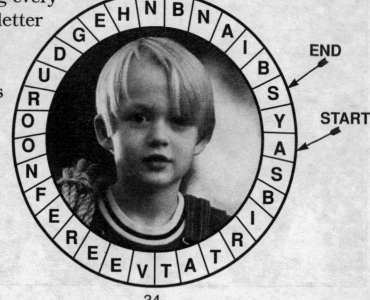

END

START

34

Mr. Wilson's Big Surprise

No one in town will baby-sit Dennis, so Dennis is going to be Mr. Wilson's houseguest for a few days.

How many words of three or more letters can you make using the letters in **HOUSEGUEST?** We found 30! Can you find more?

_____   _____
_____   _____
_____   _____
_____   _____
_____   _____
_____   _____
_____   _____
_____   _____
_____   _____

Hey Mr. Wilson!

_____   _____
_____   _____
_____   _____
_____   _____

Good Cents!

Mr. Wilson is starting to warm
up to Dennis—well, just a
little, anyway! He's showing
Dennis his priceless coin
collection. Can you tell which two coins are
exactly the same?

1   **2**   **3**   **4**   **5**

6 7 8 9 10

Bath Time!

It's bath time for Mr. Wilson's houseguest! Can you find all the bath-time words on page 39 in the puzzle below? Look up, down, forward, backward, and diagonally. Circle the words you find.

K	C	U	D	R	E	B	B	U	R
S	W	H	E	S	R	N	U	H	T
I	H	S	O	O	S	K	B	U	S
K	I	A	R	N	N	W	B	L	H
R	P	R	M	I	I	N	L	E	O
Y	I	K	S	P	L	E	E	W	W
M	T	E	L	I	O	T	B	O	E
S	S	A	I	L	B	O	A	T	R
W	A	S	H	C	L	O	T	H	L
I	K	E	A	P	R	U	H	N	E

MIRROR

SAILBOAT

SHAMPOO

SOAPY

TUB

TOWEL

WASHCLOTH

SINK

RUBBER DUCK   TOILET   SHOWER   BUBBLE BATH

Put the remaining uncircled letters in the blank spaces below, and you'll find out how Dennis knows when bath time is over!

Answer:

__ __ __ __ __   __ __ __ __

__ __ __ __

__ __ __ __ __ __ __ __ __

__ __ __ __ __ __ __ __ __ __ __ !

A Ruff Night!

While he's been staying at the Wilsons', Dennis misses Ruff something awful. He can even hear Ruff calling to him from the front yard. Can you help Ruff find Dennis?

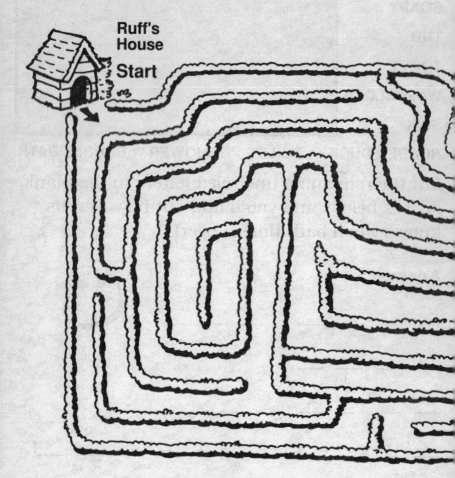

Ruff's House

Start

End

Whoops!

Mr. Wilson takes Dennis up to the attic and gets more than he bargained for—because where Dennis goes, trouble follows! When Dennis opens up a smelly old box, 32 moths escape! Can you help Dennis find them all? Circle them as you go.

MARCH

FUN GAME

43

Valuable Clues

Back at the tree house a strange man is waiting for Dennis, Joey, and Margaret. Little do they know that the stranger is really Switchblade Sam! To find out what Switchblade Sam plans to steal next, unscramble the letters and put them in the blank spaces below.

REMAGTSAR   TEMROSH   TEBS   LYEJREW

1. __ __ **R** __ __ __ __ __ **T** ' __

__ **O** __ __ __ __ ' __

__ __ __ __   **J** __ __ __ __ __ **R** __ .

YOSJE   HRATFSE   ROOLC   VOIISENETL

2. __ __ __ **Y** ' __   __ __ **T** __ __ __ __ ' __

__ __ __ __ __ __

__ **E** __ __ __ __ **S** __ __ __ .

RM   SILNOWS   DOGL   NOISC

3. __ __ .   __ __ **L** __ __ __ '

__ __ __ __ __   __ **O** __ __ __ .

44

Garden of Delight

The garden club is coming to see Mr. Wilson's prized century plant bloom for the first and last time!

Add or subtract the letter and picture clues to see what other flowers the garden club will find in Mr. Wilson's garden.

1.  – OE + U =

_____

2. D+  –CT+  – FT+ 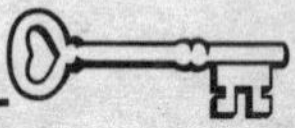 – KE =

_____

3.  – AT +  – N =

_____

4.  + ⚒ –IL + ⊙ –RE + 1 –E =

_____

5. 🐕 – OG + 🧤 –H + E + 🦁 =

_____

6. ☀ + F + 📷 –GS + 🕸 –B + R =

_____

Dennis Makes a Mess!

Martha Wilson put out some great snacks for the garden club. Too bad Dennis is there to topple the tables and send the food flying! See what Martha was going to serve. Use the clues to fill in the puzzle.

ACROSS
2. Frozen dessert.

3. Bubbly drink.

4. Chocolate chip _____.

7. Large, juicy summer fruit.

DOWN
1. Dennis can eat several peanut butter and jelly___.

5. Blow out the candles on the birthday_____.

6. This fruit comes in bunches.

8. Squirrels collect these.

Bookworm

Switchblade Sam is at it again! He's broken into Mr. Wilson's house looking for Mr. Wilson's coin collection. But Mr. Wilson has hidden it in a safe behind a phony book. Write down all the underlined letters in the book titles. Then unscramble the letters to find which fake book the safe is hidden behind.

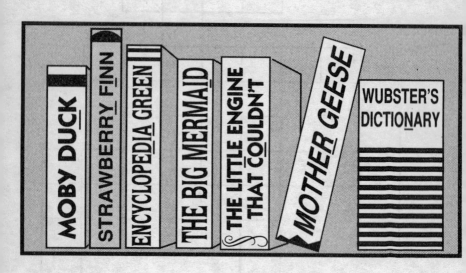

The safe is hidden behind this book:

___ ___ ___ ___ ___ ___ ___ ___ ___ ___

Who Was That?

Dennis goes to Turley's Woods after ruining Mr. Wilson's big garden-club day. But soon it turns dark, and Dennis gets scared. Can you find all these spooky night noises in the puzzle?

WHOOSH HOOT CRASH SWISH CRUNCH HOWL CACKLE SNAP EEEK

Look up, down, forward, backward, and diagonally. Circle the words you find.

```
H  R  F  C  S  H  K  L
S  Y  H  W  C  C  J  E
O  L  I  O  A  F  H  E
O  S  H  C  O  P  C  E
H  D  K  S  V  T  N  K
W  L  A  N  A  I  U  Z
E  O  O  A  M  R  R  X
O  S  H  P  C  V  C  G
N  M  L  W  O  H  D  S
```

Turley's Woods

Use the clues to fill in the puzzle.

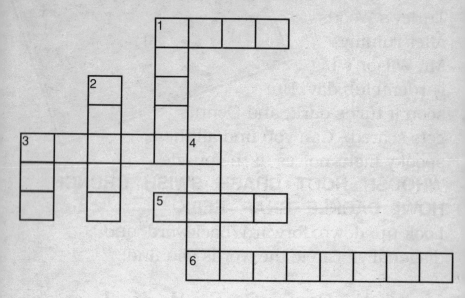

ACROSS

1. Insects that make honey.

3. Another name for woods.

5. A doe is a female_____.

6. Bushy-tailed animal.

DOWN

1. These big animals love to eat honey.

2. They often build nests in trees.

3. Sly forest animal.

4. Oak, maple, and chestnut are kinds of _____.

Lurking in the Shadows!

Uh-oh. Switchblade Sam hid in Turley's Woods to kidnap Dennis! Can you find Sam's shadow?

Sorry Sam!

Why doesn't Switchblade Sam have a chance against the Menace of Meadowmead? Cross out all the **F**'s, **G**'s, **J**'s, **K**'s, **Q**'s, **X**'s, **Y**'s, and **Z**'s and find out!

K F B X G J F E X C
A Z Y U K G S J E Y
G H E Q Q K S Z A Z
Q L K L F G Z Q F T
I K E D Z U P F F A
Y T X Q T J G H G E
F M F O Y Q M G J K
E N T X Y J G K K Y

Answer:

—— —— —— —— —— —— —— ——'——

—— —— —— —— —— —— —— ——

—— —— —— —— ——

—— —— —— —— —— ——!

Going in Circles

Everybody's been out all night looking for Dennis, but they keep going around in circles. Go around the circle twice, writing down every other letter in the blank spaces. Maybe you can help them find Dennis!

Answer:

__ __ ' __   __ __ __

__ __ __ __ __   __ __ __

__ __ __ __ __ __ __ __ __

__ __ __ .

Sam's Taking a Trip!

Switchblade Sam will never bother anyone again! Where's Sam going? Shade in all the odd-numbered spaces and find out!

Safe and Sound!

Spell out the name of each picture and put it in the boxes. When you're done, the letters in the shaded boxes will spell out the surprise the Wilsons have planned to celebrate Dennis's safe return!

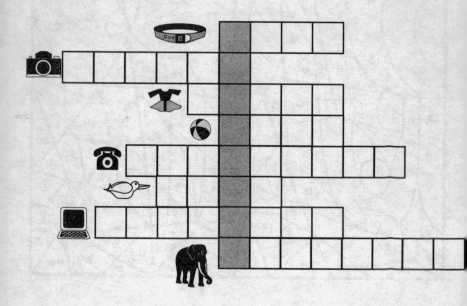

Answers

Page 3
D e n n i s
M i t c h e l l

Pages 6 and 7

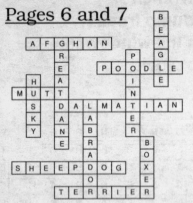

Pages 4 and 5

N	O	S	L	I	W	E	G	R	O	E	G
T	D	B	R	A	N	W	B	R	G	R	U
E	H	S	B	R	R	U	F	F	A	S	N
R	X	Z	O	O	H	A	D	M	S	P	T
A	J	O	E	Y	U	N	B	V	E	R	H
G	N	V	X	R	O	U	T	C	L	P	E
R	S	D	F	N	K	H	I	C	F	T	R
A	B	B	K	E	E	L	L	U	R	Q	Q
M	A	R	T	H	A	W	I	L	S	O	N

Pages 8 and 9
3 and 6

Pages 10 and 11
**To the Wilsons'
house to wake Mr.
Wilson!**

Page 15
A slingshot

Pages 16 and 17
1. warm 2. grades 3. hat
4. east 5. e o u
At M a r g a r e t
W a d e's h o u s e!

Pages 12 and 13

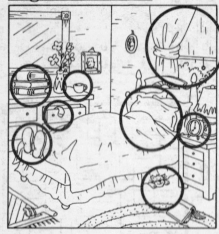

Answers

Page 18

Page 19
A tree house

Page 22
1. 2   2. 4   3. 2   4. A kite
5. A wrench
6. A dump truck
7. On the windowsill
8. 3 o'clock

Page 23
The mystery man is Switchblade Sam.

Page 24

S	D	O	M	I	N	O	E	S	W
S	R	E	K	C	E	H	C	I	T
C	R	A	Y	O	N	S	C	M	E
R	U	B	B	E	R	B	A	L	L
H	J	L	B	L	A	R	S	D	C
P	A	O	E	S	B	A	D	M	Y
O	C	C	T	L	O	O	R	K	C
T	K	K	E	B	L	A	C	B	I
Y	S	S	L	O	U	O	C	I	B
S	E	L	Z	Z	U	P	D	S	E

Page 25
Switchblade Sam took Baby Louise!

Page 26

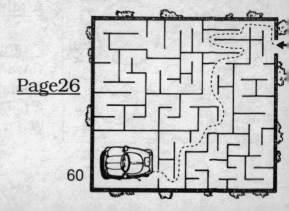

60

Answers

Page 27

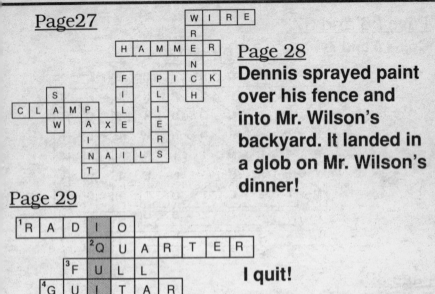

Page 28

Dennis sprayed paint over his fence and into Mr. Wilson's backyard. It landed in a glob on Mr. Wilson's dinner!

Page 29

I quit!

Pages 30 and 31 Chewing gum and glue

Pages 32 and 33

1. diamonds 2. cash 3. tools 4. apple 5. wallet
6. money 7. television   D̲e̲n̲n̲i̲s̲ M̲i̲t̲c̲h̲e̲l̲l̲

Page 34

A brave enough baby-sitter for Dennis!

Page 35

(possible answers) hoe, hose, hot, house, hug, hut, get, ghost, goes, got, guess, guest, gust, gut, out, see, set, she, sheet, shoes, shout, shut, south, the, these, toe, tug, toss, thug, hog...

Answers

Page 36 and 37
Coins 4 and 7

Page 38

```
K C U D R E B B U R
S W H E S R N U H T
I H S O O S K B U S
K I A R N W B L H
R P R M I N E W O
Y I K S P L E W E
M T E L I O T B O R
S S A I L B O A T
W A S H C L O T H
I K E A P R U H N E
```

Page 39

**When his skin
wrinkles like a prune!**

Pages 40 and 41

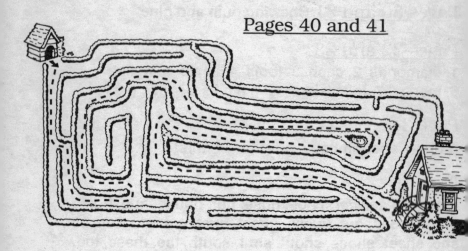

Answers

Pages 42 and 43

Page 44

1. Margaret's mother's best jewelry.
2. Joey's father's color television.
3. Mr. Wilson's gold coins.

Pages 46 and 47

1. Tulips 2. Daisy 3. Rose 4. Carnation
5. Dandelion 6. Sunflower

Page 49

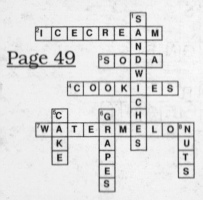

Page 50

D i c t i o n a r y

Page 51

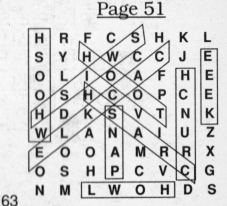

Answers

Page 52

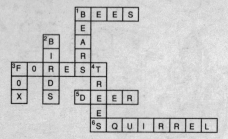

Page 53
Shadow 4

Page 55
Because he's all tied up at the moment!

Page 56
He's in the woods with Switchblade Sam.

Page 57
To Jail

Page 58

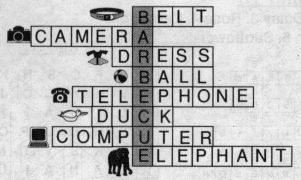